S0-ABC-713

DATE DUE

AG 28 '95	JUL 2 9 95	
NO 04 '95	DEC 4	
NO 30 '95		
AP 8 '96		
JUN 3 1 '96		
AG 0 8 '96		
OCT 3 1 '96		
WITHDRAWN		

Demco, Inc. 38-293

Good Morning, Pond

Alyssa Satin Capucilli

ILLUSTRATED BY Cynthia Jabar

Hyperion Books for Children
New York

TOWN OF ORANGE
PUBLIC LIBRARY
ORANGE, CONN.

jP/c

Text © 1994 by Alyssa Satin Capucilli.
Illustrations © 1994 by Cynthia Jabar.
All rights reserved.

Printed in the United States of America.
For information address Hyperion Books for Children,
114 Fifth Avenue, New York, New York 10011.
FIRST EDITION
1   3   5   7   9   10   8   6   4   2

Library of Congress Cataloging-in-Publication Data
Capucilli, Alyssa
Good morning, pond/by Alyssa Satin Capucilli; illustrated by
Cynthia Jabar—1st ed.
p.   cm.
Summary: The leap of a little green frog signals the start of a
new day as the creatures of the pond awake and go through a variety
of morning rituals.
ISBN 1-56282-674-3 (trade)—ISBN 1-56282-675-1 (lib. bdg.)
[1. Ponds—Fiction.   2. Pond animals—Fiction.   3. Morning—
Fiction.   4. Stories in rhyme.]   I. Jabar, Cynthia, ill.
II. Title.
PZ8.3.C1935Go   1994
[E]—dc20   93-29311   CIP   AC

The artwork for each picture is prepared using watercolor and ink.
This book is set in 18-point Goudy Old Style.

102123

ribbit

To my family…and especially for
Peter, Laura, and Billy,
who love the pond
—A.S.C.

For Neil and Cecilia with love
—C.J.

When a little green frog jumps up with a leap,
it's wake-up time at the pond!

When a little green frog jumps up with a leap
and splashes the fish who were fast asleep,

splash

it's wake-up time at the pond!

glub

glub

glub

When a little green frog jumps up with a leap
and splashes the fish who were fast asleep
and the fish swim off with a wave of their tails
and out of the sand crawl a pair of snails,

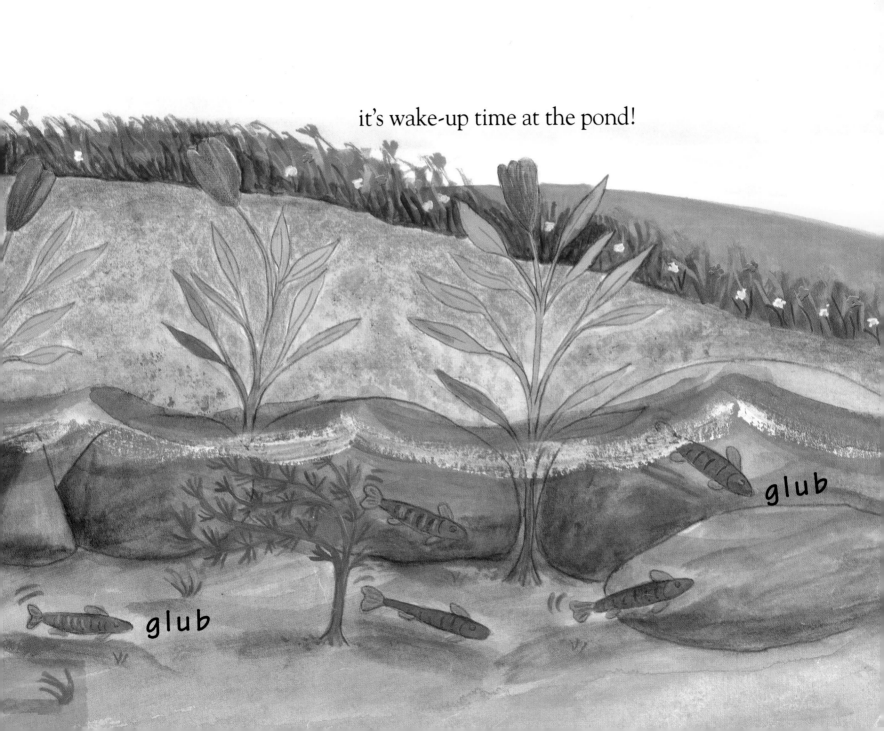

When red salamanders begin to stir,
it's stretching time at the pond!

When red salamanders begin to stir
and grasshoppers spring with a hum and a whir,

hum

hum

whir

it's stretching time at the pond!

TOWN OF ORANGE
PUBLIC LIBRARY
ORANGE, CONN.

When red salamanders begin to stir
and grasshoppers spring with a hum and a whir,
when out from his shell a turtle peeks
at the hungry birds who open their beaks,

it's stretching time at the pond!

When dragonflies hover on buzzing wings,
it's singing time at the pond!

When dragonflies hover on buzzing wings
as "croak-croak-croak!" an old toad sings,

it's singing time at the pond!

croak

croak

croak

When dragonflies hover on buzzing wings
as "croak-croak-croak!" an old toad sings,
when ducks paddle by with a "quack-quack-quack!"
and "honk-honk-honk!" the geese answer back,

When little feet tiptoe through grass wet with dew,
it's sneaking time at the pond!

When big eyes watch and ears listen, too,
it's peeking time at the pond!

When chins rest in hands and bellies lie still,
when the golden sun spreads morning light on the hill . . .

when soft white clouds go tumbling by
in the new day's bright awakening sky…

Wake up, stretch, sing…
good morning, pond!

splash

TOWN OF ORANGE
PUBLIC LIBRARY
ORANGE, CONN.